Theodore's Plate

A Christmas Fable by
Stephen Wade Nebgen

Illustrated by
Jonathan Fitzgibbons

World Castle Publishing, LLC

Pensacola, FL

Copyright © Stephen Wade Nebgen 2019

Hardback ISBN: 9781950890729

Paperback ISBN: 9781950890736

eBook ISBN: 9781950890743

First Edition World Castle Publishing, LLC, October 14, 2019

http://www.worldcastlepublishing.com

Licensing Notes

Illustrator: Jonathan Fitzgibbons

THANK YOU

"Everything, always, for Jill, Austin, and Lindsay."

- Stephen

"To my family, for being my constant source of support and inspiration."

- Jonathan

ACKNOWLEDGEMENTS

Stephen Wade Nebgen: Mom and Dad; Austin and Lindsay Nebgen; Mark Nebgen & Susan Cosley-Harvey; Don, Pam and Qin Nebgen; Matt, Brenda, Drew and Hailey Nebgen; Steve & Joy Carmichael; Peter Grahame & Henry Seale; Ken Waissman; Ellen Canacakos; Pete Angelus; Jan Caraway; Carole Bartholomeaux; Sharon Schmitz; James and June Hagen; Kevin and Nancy McCarthy; Robert Alpert; Lisa Stapp; Bruno Walter; Erik Shein; and Karen Fuller.

Jonathan Fitzgibbons: "Mom, Grandpa, Grandma, my siblings Bill and Emily Miller, and our pup BJE."

4

Before you start reading this book, get some hot chocolate, climb into bed with Mommy or Daddy, and snuggle up close and warm and cozy in your blankets.

Are you ready? Ok, let's start the story!

It was Christmas Eve and the snow had been falling all night. It blanketed the branches on the trees and filled the path.

The snow stuck to the King's thick beard and the heavy cloak he wore.

The King pushed on, intent on a secret mission that would bring peace to his kingdom.

He continued to trudge through the snow, head bowed.

In the small cottage, the family gathered around the fireplace. It was a large family, with the father and mother, and three sons and three daughters.

The family was poor and the most precious belonging of the family was a set of beautiful plates – one for each member of the family. The plates had been made by a local potter in exchange for work by the father.

The plates were only used at the big holidays, such as Christmas and Easter.

On these days, the father would catch a wild pheasant and the mother would go to the root cellar and get potatoes, onions, beets, pumpkins, and cabbage. For them, it would be a feast!

But three years before, the littlest one, Theodore, had slipped when going back to his place at the table, and his plate had broken!

The father said, "Oh, Theodore!"

The mother said, "Oh, Theodore!"

The children all said, "Oh, Theodore!"

The father had managed to fix the plate, but everyone felt it was not as beautiful as before.

Theodore always had to use the broken plate at the holidays, and it was always at the bottom of the stack of the plates.

Then, there was a loud banging at the door!

The father went to see who was there. He opened the door, and the King stood outside with snow covering his beard and his face. The father did not recognize the King.

The King said, "May I have food and lodging for the evening?"

The father said, "Of course, but we only have a simple dinner.

The King said, "That will be fine and thank you so very much!"

The mother ladled out the food from the large pot hanging over the fire.

The father went first, presenting his beautiful plate. The oldest child came next and then each child in their turn. Theodore was the last of the children.

After Theodore, came the King. The mother had given the King an old wooden bowl to eat from. The mother ladled some food into the wooden bowl

King said, "Thank you so much for your generosity."

The mother said, "You are more than welcome. Have more if you wish."

The King went to the table. The mother then ladled food onto her plate.

After a simple blessing, the father, the mother, and each of the children started to eat. But Theodore hesitated for a minute and looked at the King. Theodore stood up with his broken plate that was filled with food and walked around the table to the King.

Theodore said, "Here, sir, you can use my plate to eat and I will eat from the bowl."

Theodore handed the plate of food to the King.

The King said, "But that is your plate! Are you sure you want to give it to me?"

Theodore said, "Yes, sir. I am sorry that the plate was broken!"

The King said, "That is the most wonderful gift I could have received this Christmas! It may have been broken once but not now. It is a beautiful plate!"

Then, even though there were no real presents, the family would sit around the fire and each child was given a chance to say what gift they would want.

The children loved this moment when they could dream fantastic thoughts and go to magical places. Theodore had always wished to have a falcon! He loved the soaring, speedy bird.

In the morning, everyone woke up and ate breakfast.

The King then made his way to the secret meeting place with the other King and they spoke for a long time. After that, they shook hands and agreed on peace for their respective kingdoms.

The King made his way back to his kingdom and to his castle. The King made the great announcement of peace and the people started to cheer that it was now here! And on Christmas Day!

But the King was a bit troubled. He could not forget the family that had shown him such generosity. And they did not even know he was their King!

The family's generosity was pure and simple and without regard for a reward.

He told his knights and attendants to get presents together for the family. New tools for the father, pots and pans for the mother, a special gift for each child according to the wish that each had described.

And for Theodore, he had a special gift. The package was not a box but something with a cover over it. The King mounted his horse and took the package onto his saddle. The King, the knights, and the attendants turned down the path that led to the family's cottage.

In the cottage, the loud sound of horses and men and clanging metal could be heard!

The family stood and went to the door to see what could be making such a sound.

They walked out in front of the cottage and saw a spectacle in front of them!

The King, the knights, and the attendants had all gathered in front of the cottage!

The King got down from his horse and handed the covered package to his attendant.

The King walked to the father. The father said, "Good King... but... but... you were here last night! Oh my King, did we insult you in some way?"

The King, "No, kind sir. You and your family gave me the greatest gift that I have ever received. You did so much for me and my kingdom!

"And, so in return, I have brought you presents. Each is something that you dreamed of and spoke about last night!"

Excited, all the children opened their gifts but nothing had been given to Theodore.

The father said, "Dear King, I do not mean to be bold but did you have a present for Theodore?"

The King said, "Of course. A special one and here it is!"

The attendant brought the covered package to the King. The King took the package and with a big flourish, raised the cover. There, in a beautiful birdcage, was a falcon!

The King said, "My attendant shall teach you how to train the falcon to hunt for you and to come back to you. The falcon shall become your friend and protector."

Theodore said, "I shall love this falcon with all my heart! Thank you, dear King."

The King said, "In all of my kingdom, this is the richest home I know. God bless you all and peace be with you!"

The King and the knights and the attendants all mounted and turned and headed back to the castle. The family waved as the King disappeared over the hill.

The sun went down and the family gathered by the fireplace, marveling at their wonderful Christmas gifts.

Theodore was especially happy and watched the falcon soar in the air.

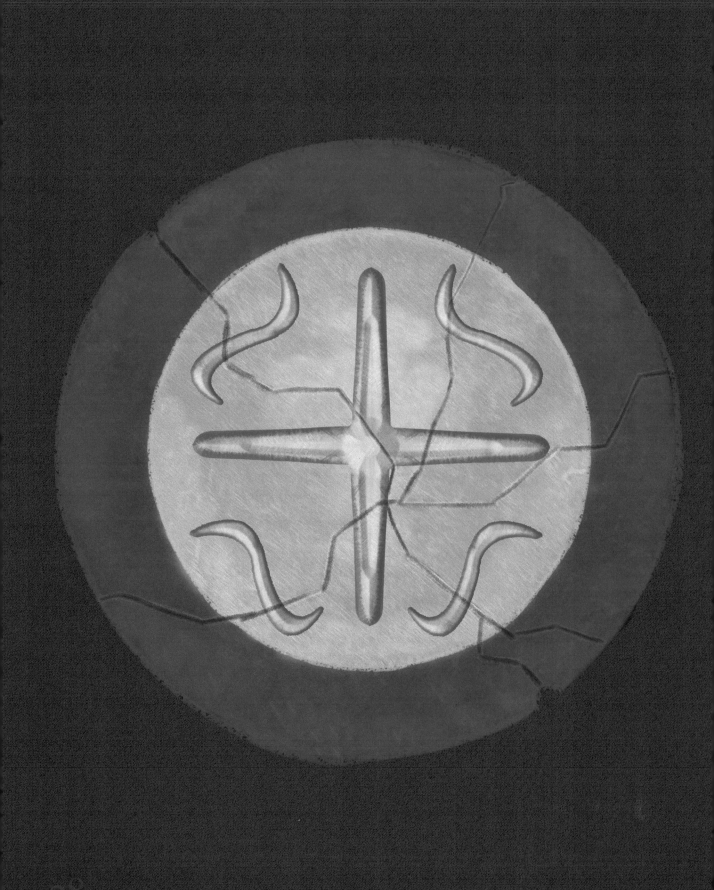

Going inside, Theodore then saw his plate with the other plates in the special place that they were kept, but now his plate was on top of the stack!

About the Author and Illustrator

Stephen Wade Nebgen, a single father of two and entertainment attorney, created THEODORE'S PLATE for his two children and his beloved late wife, Jill. Mr. Nebgen has been a producer, director and writer, and has numerous credits in film, theatre and television. However, his labor of love for his children and late wife is THEODORE'S PLATE.

JONATHAN FITZGIBBONS has been working as a contract 3D artist/game designer since 2017. Outside of his main profession, he enjoys pursuing a wide variety of activities ranging from animation to improvisational comedy. Theodore's Plate is his first foray into book illustrations, and he looks forward to contributing his artwork in future literary works.

CPSIA information can be obtained
at www.ICGtesting.com
Printed in the USA
BVHW021345301019
562432BV00003BA/3/P